Fanfiction: Harry Potter's Verse

Poetry of a Magician

Adam Smith

ISBN: 9781976955679
Imprint: Independently published

DEDICATION

I thank my mother for giving me life.

And thanks to all of you folks who are reading my books.

Shallow nights begun with wind,
I stand here in a form of a dog,
And pretend that not even god,
Can move me from my keep.
And I let the other dogs laugh at me
As I am carried away to battle,
the darkness and it's friends.

Defenses are tight,
We are standing against fierce army,
Of angry dwarfs,
We've been hated for being magical kind,
But this battle shows no mercy even to the mightiest wizard minds.

You can blame it on the spell books,
You can blame it on the teacher,
But I blame it on myself, hood,
I blame it on myself, cause I wasn't right,
Not even tonight.

Journey into the dark part of the woods,
Brings a lot of things that are misunderstood.
There are Ents and creatures not described in any books,
Of muggles or even magic,
The terror, if you are without a wand, or a skill
Is unmeasurable.
But I journey not alone,
A giant servant is with me,
Keeping the spirits high and my mind strong.

Harsh and cold is the weather at our battle fort,
I just wish you to see.
Open your eyes and be with me,
The cold will turn to warmth,
And you will see how easier the life will be.

6

Broken wand,
Broken spirit,
I wish I've had enough of merit,
To fix the broken spirit.
When everything goes wrong,
It means you're going through a black stripe in your life.
Carry on because the white one is ahead,
If will surprise you, so better remain alive than dead.

7

Break me not,
I'm a magician!
A wizard,
Half god,
I'm of great use,
To those who understand,
And keep their world at soothe and in sync,
With those just like me.

8

I want to present you with a flower,
It has an enormous power,
To bend the reality towards your own desires,
Let us agree that it is what most hearts of men require.

9

Silence! Listen!
There is an indifferent condition,
I want to burn down entire town,
The Russian, the English, the Jews.
I want to see it burn to ashes,
Because none of these are worthy the love,
I had towards the girl who listened to blouse.
The magical sound that created this town,
In matter of minutes, it turned my soul,
Into something worth keeping and not just ignored.
Now that she is gone,
I hear only silence,
And only search for bottles of whiskeys and wines.

10

Dungeon and its secrets,
The concrete swarming with little hostile rats,
I pretend I couldn't be fooled or led,
My magic wand still glowing with strength,
And it shows me the safest way though,
I am concerned, and it is the least I can say,
But today I might not make it home before the dusk anyway.

11

People know a little bit about each and every one,
I can admit, I was surprised by profound knowledge,
That was shared with me,
But I was not the only one,
Time and time again life proved me that magic happens,
When you less than slightly understand it.

Who wants to drop dead?
Not me, that's certainly.
Who wants to be admired for genius in art?
Certainly, count me.
That's why it is so hard to get the things that are desired?
I doubt you know the answer that is required.
But I will conquer my fear, and step on that stage,
To give the concert and forge my way,
To be.

You never learned from Adam Smith.
You choose money over love,
And pretend you know all the secrets.
The possibility is dull,
You only know yourself,
And even that is dull.
Go learn thyself and be better than any fool.

Walking late at night,
At the castle's library.
Searching for a tome,
To ease my misery.
Searching for the wisdom,
To bring me back my sleep,
And knowledge to defend,
Myself from grip of that evil world.

15

Dark thoughts,
Have gathered in her head,
She was wondering about the dead.
And nearly headless Nick,
Was flying around her neck,
I whispered "Wake up my dear",
And she woke up.
Her rather tough dreams,
Loosened their grasp over her body and soul.

16

The depth of the labyrinth,
That lead me the to the goblet,
Was insanely deeper than any magical closet.
Some find Narnia on other end of theirs,
I find an invisible cloak at end of mine.
And Vol de Mort whispers his hissings,
He desperately hopes I will be wrong
And lose my mind to surrender to him too.

17

I'm a joke,
A chosen one.
A one who will undergo,
A great amount of torture,
Before the world will stop and it all will be gone.

Misery and sanity,
Aren't two good old friends.

I rarely encourage my fears,
To shape a picture in my head,
But now the picture appears and it appears,
To me that I'm not completely dead.
I just wander in a desert in hopes to find a well,
A good reason to bid all my misfortunes
One last courageous farewell and to keep running,
Towards the final goal.

All jokes aside,
We wish to dance this last dance,
With our wands and battle stances,
We are here to fight for lives of all that is magical,
And as miraculous as a flying car,
Or hippogriffs and northern star.
We are here to stand the stand against darkness,
All that we need to do with our charms,
And be as much righteous or
As magic can allow to fight the darkest of the darkest in this realm,
In this show.

19

I'm falling down,
Into the darkness,
I'm falling up,
Into the wildness,
I just want to be part of something,
That is closer to kindness.
Why all the magic,
Won't turn the world
Into a better place?
Why all the swords are left,
To make me face my own case?

20

Take my spell book away,
Take my magic wand too,
Take all the artifacts that I ever found,
Take all the glitter too!
I will remain with my mind sharp as a needle,
With grace of Patronus I will depart to a better place,
I will defeat my enemies by standing strong.
My own two hands are well enough strong.
I will beat all the darklings with my own head.

21

The journey through an ice cold night,
Through the winter's might,
Through the glare and flare of white,
The silence is clear,
As clear is the sight.
The enemy is near,
We have to be diligent,
We have to be right.

22

Once at the battlefield,
We shout and direct our spells at each other.
We deflect the deadly spells away from hearts,
Of our friends, toward the hearts of our foes.
It is such thing, war,
There is no mercy,
There is no peace,
There is just cruelty,
No man can retreat in one piece.

23

"Avada Kedavra"
Shouts Malfoy and directs to me,
And vivid trace of fog and flick outgo,
From his dark colored wand,
The spell would reach me, and it's strike would be fatal,
Unless I wouldn't shield myself.
"Protego" - utter my lips, and so the death,
Has no way to reach me through this strike.
We battle more, before somebody throws a mere stone,
And it hits Malfoy's forehead.
He loses consciousness but he is not dead,
A mere stone prevented a fatal outcome, of one of us.
A stone, preventing death, when higher forces are at hands,
Now fate does have a sense of humor,
The battle though continues, while other wizards grab their take,
While Malfoy rests without knowing, what was or will be his own fate.

While being young doesn't count as a story,
Being a young magician does.
Having a mark from death itself on your forehead,
Is no mystery to the magic world,
But sure is a sight for the Muggles,
Who don't understand the eccentric ways of magic words.
And phrase "I rather be marked by death than dead" shoots them
Stunned and they take it hard to understand,
Why anybody would be at all, dead.

25

Poet of death, with wand and stress,
I march my long march to pub.
To drink me some ale,
I wish I could focus on a role,
Of the magic, while I'm half-drunk
And levitating in that forgotten by the God pub...

26

My dear flying ford,
You take me higher and closer to the Lord,
Right now, I am soaring,
And observing our land.
Oh, glory!
To every little being and every little creature,
They might be scared of magic,
But mine is not so vicious
It's rather peaceful and precious!

27

Poetry and word,
It's all sacred to the Devil and to the Lord!
It's like magic to those who know it's taste,
But now I better show my skills and go,
"Alohomora" and the door is unlocked,
I walk to it and leave behind me, only fog.

28

I rest somewhere in France,
With my beloved Ginny.
And three kids!
It's fine air for quidditch,
Or a simple jog,
I find this rally rather happy ending
And therefore I'm enjoying every bit of it.

29

Archery of the Japan, it has some magic too!
You got to close your eyes,
Listen to your own heart and point the arrow,
Then you open the eyes and let it go.
When you hit the target, it symbolizes the end,
Of little scene from entire show.
As above so is below.

30

A Telegram from Daily Prophet,
I find out that somebody is dead.
Someone of minor importance,
But he was rather beheaded by a mage,
And his head carries a mark as my own,
A lightning, but I can figure it was made after the crime took place.
And so, I find this letter, and it is full of concern,
It pledges for help in solving this gruesome mystery,
And I must carry on.

31

I journey throughout the time,
In wilderness of fate,
I look around and follow,
The steps of all great men.
I know that life is not a life,
Without sorrow,
Therefor I try to worry less,
And leave behind me as little pain as I can.

One fine journey, begun long ago,
When one special child was born,
And death knocked on his door,
Mother's love saved him,
And nothing more.
Mother's love saved us all.

People ask for retribution for their enemies,
I ask for only one thing,
That I think it counts more,
I ask that all the bad jinx would miss all my friends.
And I will be the one who prevails over the darkness
For sure.

One last time,
I saw you somewhere,
Now I don't desire,
To admit.
I was there, looking for it,
Looking to quit.
Now I know what to do,
I know where are you,
And I will be there,
Wherever you decide to shop,
I will be there to lock, your pain away,
And keep it a at bay till your hair turns gray.

People think and admire,
All they can comprehend.
However magic,
Is of different desire,
It's of unexplainable mystery, passion and fire.

36

They call Mister Potter,
I survived death many times,
I am great at quidditch and fighting trolls.
My forum is little,
But everyone recognizes me,
And almost everyone knows,
I fight demons who know magic,
Cause I know magic well enough,
To fight magic with magic too.

37

When you spit on morals,
And require respect by brute force,
I'm standing there,
Guarding the law,
Protecting the weak,
With strength given to me
By the magic and knowledge
Before the darkness had stand or a lore.

38

Phoenix, magnificent bird!
Turns into fire and gives itself birth.
Wondrous fit,
For someone who needs to be fed, just to eat.

39

"Back to Hogwarts!" - would be nice thing to say,
However I am an adult, and that's my children that can say:
"Back to Hogwarts!" and leave me and Ginny in a dismay.

Long story short,
It's where begins the road.
My magic wand has chosen me,
And I know that the art chooses the artist,
Not vice versa.
We shall care our duties with outmost grace,
Everyone and each one of us, has his own place
In the magic of arts.

The darkness of the night, when moon and sun collide,
We see the creatures that are odd,
And see the hidden gold.
Only us, the bearers of magic force,
May take control of state of mind,
And bend the nature to our desire,
Such is the ever burning fire.

People travel from house to work,
From work to house,
We call it normal life.
But magic makes it more exciting,
And far more nice.
I can travel in an instance from hearth to hearth,
As I'm son of Potters, and magic runs in every cell
Of my Potter blood.

43

The power of will,
And power of want,
It takes much more,
Than mere knowledge to know
What is what.
First you get an insight,
And power of will, comes in handy,
It pushes you further to achieve what you want.
The want comes as a glimpse, as a desire,
Result of seduction of the mind, and it's born in the heart.
Such is the difference between the two,
Depends on the magic you do, which one is right for you?

44

On the wall there is a spider,
It's crawling higher up towards the warmth of a lamp,
I've spotted it cause it's as big as my palm!
And it's not a mere spider,
It's mister Gatsby!
Waiting for us to speak up,
So he could deliver to his mob
What we had to say on this meeting
In a hut in the woods of the dog.

45

Golden tooth,
Is full of magic.
Magic and a metal that never corrodes,
Are a combination of extraordinary traits,
You may experience pain when they put in your jaw,
But it does wonders, when you chew veggies and meat,
Adding the juiciness to the taste, and the feeling
Of self-washing mouth.
Before you go to sleep there are wondrous effects
Of entire experiment of living and breathing intact,
With some magic in your digestive tract.

Going back to the stars,
Our souls play their final parts,
And descend into the skies.
Such is the wonder,
When a magician dies.

Music and cassettes,
They play their old songs,
But in magical world, the tune is always new.
There are band recordings,
But bands are tired of playing the same old songs,
So they play different sounds when you turn them on
So is the magic of music in my little world.

Bandits are dangerous men,
When there is magic as their weapon of choice.
Their danger is doubled, cause they are no longer simple men.
We fight them courageously, when they try to rob our houses and banks,
But there are bandits that have invisibility cloaks, hats and socks,
Now these fellows life to the story, they are invincible invisible glory,
Up until the moment when we mark them with paint,
And then we take away their wands and put them behind the bars.

Times used to be different,
And I understand,
That world changes rapidly,
And we, magical representatives
Of this universe, have to adapt,
Life is a courageous leap of hope,
Not a graceful walk at a park.

50

Sleep is a time of a recovery,
Don't neglect your dreams,
They are messages of the brain,
And simulations of what could have been.
Dream and see the worlds that are beyond,
Our expectations,
Such is the magic of sleep.

51

Every day,
We get swayed away.
Every time,
Something new,
Comes to mind,
Before we know it.
And it turns into magic,
Like a morning dew,
We don't expect it,
But it's there, makes us happy
And wet if we step on it at the morning,
As squirrels and cats do.

52

Azkaban is a prison for outlaw wizards,
Where Dementors torture their prey.
I wish uncle Sirius Black,
Wouldn't ever end up there.
His vision and his stare,
Are full of despair,
Still appear in front of me.
His death is not in vain,
He died as hero, and sparkle of his light
Will always bring warmth to my heart.

When you dream about her,
Don't forget the magic you couldn't ignore,
Don't forget the truth she taught you as a play,
Don't forget her.
What her smile brought you when you used to smile
And say "Hey Hermione, how are you today?"

Windows full of flame,
Usually it's an end of a game,
Fire consumes us all.

There is yet something,
Something magical in my soul,
And I wish to see life a bit more,
Therefor I jump and scream out
"Expeco Patronum" to let my father's spirit
Carry me through my difficult way.

I used to be a little boy,
With passion for every new charm.
My question was only one,
How to survive?
How to remain a whole, a one?

But time has passed,
I succeeded in every battle and war,
I don't need to fight anymore.

56

Sitting in my parlor,
Wondering, how our world could get more,
Of sun,
Of happiness,
Of Ale,
And of peace?
As a Potter, I have questions,
That never decrease.

57

The pain you feel from a broken bone,
While playing quidditch –
Is nothing in comparison to pain you feel
When losing good friend.

58

If you don't like what you do,
You better stay away from yourself for a day or two,
You will find and learn a thing or two
About what you should really do.

59

Every wizard knows to say
"Hello",
Every wizard knows to say
"Hello",
I just fantasize about my way
To the big show.
I fantasize about my day,
And muggle wizard war.
I see the sky and the sea,
Today is another day to stay alive,
And try to be free.

Locked in a room?
Use "Alohomora" and ride the broom,
I personally was happy to receive my Nimbus 2000
Back in the first grade,
Such things aren't forgotten.
Even if, the memory turns out to be a little delayed,
Such is the magic,
Of expression,
First impression
And life that moves us on.

Silence drives mad even the strongest of us,
But it's better to be in silence than to be dead.
Astute is the magic of silence,
Astute is the magic of yore,
All we wish is a binding agreement,
With power we try of absorb.

Dark valleys and dark arts,
Suspicion tears us apart.
We walk through the darkness,
Under the light of our own spells,
We find misery and destruction,
That could be seen only in hell.

Peaceful time,
Peaceful rhyme,
The war is over, Voldemort is gone.
Season of healing is on,
Season of sun.

64

Sun and moon,
Give us a natural light.
One is at day the other at night.
Magic spells cannot affect them,
But they affect magic with ease.
I hope good powers, with sun, will increase
As the darkness will surrender to the light of the moon.
Such is my will, before night, before noon.

65

I try to be as least remarkable as possible,
I'm tired of giving out a fight,
My fate, I believe holds more for me,
Than magical battles, and persistent need to be right.

66

Biblical, magical,
Starling, ice breaking, strategical.
I wish for peace and clarity,
I wish for better world,
If magic is the key,
I draw my wand and sharpen my sword.

67

Epos is written by heroic deeds,
My epos is made with help of my friends,
And good amount of pious deeds.
Safety of life and fear of death,
Give us courage to keep on, to progress.

Merit and mercy,
Are equal fits.
Which we have to practice,
To be living and not to be dead or obsolete.
Life makes some changes,
So is the magic,
But merit and mercy,
Aren't measured by fate,
They are measured by choice and by mindful grace,
You carry them out and try to obey.

Rising above the enemies,
Be they magical creatures, wizards of muggles,
All of them are united by hate towards you,
Standalone wizard with name and courage,
Trying to defeat demons who want make you into a porridge,
Be you willing or not to defeat them with magic and sorcery.

Wish not for ability to discern,
The good from the evil.
But rather for ability to be concerned,
With magical power that brings the upheaval.

Art or heart,
Nothing will make us part.
We are together in this,
For better or worse,
We will carry further, regardless,
The noise, voice or spell.
We are together,
Cause we know that otherwise there is no good but only hell.

71

The winter,
The snow,
Everybody has to know,
Where is the magic coming from,
Be it a wand,
Or magician's heart,
We are loyal to the magical art.

72

Ginny making me breakfast,
Lily and James playing cards.
Albus trying to throw magical darts,
I sit and read Daily Prophet.
Nothing else could be better than this
Moment of warm life,
This is true magic,
True magic of light.

73

Gaming and naming,
We play good old games, in my family.
And we give names to our adversaries while doing so.
Quidditch is the most fun topic we get to talk about,
While at home.
I miss good old days when I used to be the Quidditch hound,
Now, my kids are playing the game,
In a name,
In a name.

Negative thoughts drift in the cloud,
And in a smog,
I can feel the darkness takes its place,
In heads of the dwellers of London,
And all around.
We should be careful, cause,
Darkness knows when we are afraid.
We should carry our wands and our minds,
Ready for whatever it is that to come.
Give or take.

I miss the old flying ford,
It was such an awesome invention!
Flying with style while muggles,
Squabble upon the ground,
In an enormous tension.

Dragons and Spiders,
Hagrid used to have them all.
After all he was half giant,
And he needed something to keep him warm.
Living all alone in the woods,
Makes you feel feelings,
To those creatures who are generally misunderstood.
Such is the way of the dark wood,
And the hut that makes you brood.

Magical clouds,
Sky, and all that it surrounds.
The atmosphere
I've heard there are magical beasts,
Who make it rain.
This is fantastic,
Absolutely insane!
That's why, in London, we have so much rain.

78

Time is not a circle, neither it's a triangle,
Or square,
Time is a spiral,
And moves in spiral way,
I only wish I have enough time,
To say "I love you",
In every possible way.

79

Hippogriffs magnificent noble beasts,
I remember how I used to fly one,
When I wore younger man clothes.
And I must say,
You better do it at least once in your life,
Than doing it only in the depth of your soul.

80

Fighting the Troll,
Was funny adventure from the very start.
We were at the first magical grade,
And beaten that monster with a mere wand.
Almost no magic,
But we succeeded from the beginning, from the very start.
I cherish the memory of Ron, Hermione, and I
Fighting that fight,
It could be dark, but it turned out alright.

Nothing left to win,
And nothing left to lose,
All I need is magic, and potions
Not to feel bruised.
I can see it in your eyes,
People did not have to tell me lies,
Death is coming slowly,
To those who are about to die,
I just wish I could stay a little longer,
And give a life another try.

I just summoned a little magical creature,
Into its own way,
All I wish is now to say,
How have you never planned it, and did not say,
That you want magical creature where you now stay?
I just wish for better love,
For better mind,
I just wish for it to be inclined,
I wish for middle way,
Such is my magical day.

It's an obsession,
To seek for magical protection.
All I really need, is a bit of time with my family,
Loving Ginny, Albus, Lily and James,
All I need is these three little magical saints.

Now you see me,
Now you don't,
Invisibility is one of my main goals.
I try to do it my best,
That is, to your life without rest,
Restless strife to succeed,
Restless need to be magically fit.

85

Prayer is good,
I'm a wizard but I still believe in God,
Somebody brought magic into this world,
So I sometimes go into that hall,
And pray for us all, to keep going on.

86

I'm not alone, the ash is falling upon me.
And I know that I have to move on,
Science is advancing, and the world of magic trembling,
I just need to go on, and rediscover who I am,
And what should make me go on.
I know that, now - is what we should cherish.
Our life has an end,
And you should know that wherever you stand,
You are your own most valuable friend.

87

Everyone has to have a job, to make it.
Otherwise, the life will try and make you break it.
I just work at Aurora, Ministry of Magic,
We made couple of changes since the battle of Hogwarts,
And people say they like what we do,
I hope you do too.

88

I no longer can talk to the snakes,
This magical power abandoned me.
Now, all I do when I see a snake,
Is try to bot step on it.
And hold my wand with "Alarte Ascendare"
Prepared to launch it away.

So many stars are there at the sky,
I wonder what magic they possess,
And how they affect us when we die?
And turn indo stardust when we are no longer, a mess.

90

Dudley grew up to be a good fellow.
We now meet sometimes with our families,
Sometimes you shouldn't judge the person by his past,
Sometimes you ought to let past have a rest.

91

You act like you never happened.
And I think to myself,
That we are one but not the same,
Now let's continue that game.
I care for my love,
But do you know, what are you carrying for?
After all we are one but not the same,
This is the essence of this weird game.

92

My bullet proof cloak,
Makes me drop all other defenses down,
All I want is to see a world
Where there is no need in magic to feel like a magician,
Or be with a face that is frown.

93

I can't handle it,
I got my candle lit,
Now as I go,
I understand and I know,
That talent has always time to grow,
As wizard to wizard believe me I know.

94

Is it getting better,
When you call me by name.
You got someone to shame,
All I know and all I'm wishing for,
Is a simple merit in this game.

Let us grow,
And climb higher than the doves can fly,
I want to see winter and invent a new name,
For this game we are playing in a name of,
In a name of somebody saint.

95

Want to run a way,
Back home where I can play,
Back to being young,
When magic was magic and not just an art,
Now I know how it is,
To be grown up and make your own breeze,
I will never let my life freeze,
All I want Ginny, is you.

96

Threw away all the lies,
But couldn't take your heart.
This is the life,
This is the art.

97

Standing bare foot, in the rain,
Waiting for it to pass,
I summon the rainbow,
And make it to the past,
To see the life again and learn to adjust.

Let's keep our hands together,
No matter the weather,
Let's keep on singing our little songs,
Our spells, our wands, our cards and our dolls.
I want to see you walking and running when the rest just
Know how to crawl and bow to the Gods they made before
They were even known.

Britain is here,
Sleeps under magical spell,
Dreams come and go,
But Britain is here,
It's letting you grow,
Letting you know where one of us
Should go,
And we let him go.

One last thing I have to say,
Before I part with you and return to my way,
I want to say "Thank you",
For having the courage to wonder throughout my thoughts,
My visions and dreaming, that is very odd,
I wish you farewell
And may the magic be with you,
As is the spell.

Thank you for reading this book. I hope you have enjoyed it and have gained something for yourself along the way. I want to wish you well along the road of life.

If you would, please leave a review for this book. People like to know what other people think, and if you could be so kind and let them know, I would remain forever grateful.

For more of my works, you may visit my website:
www.dragonpoe.com

.

Or the Amazon Author Page: amazon.com/author/sirsmith

For personal inquiries, write me at welshdragonmcmillan@gmail.com

Thank you.

Truly yours,

Adam Smith

ABOUT THE AUTHOR

Adam Prockstem Smith is an entrepreneur, blogger, and an international author. At the age of sixteen, he started his first business building one-page internet marketing websites. He speaks fluent Russian, Hebrew, and English.

After finishing high school, he proceeded with self-education and exploration of the nature of the human mind. Through extensive research, and many trials and errors, Adam has become experienced with Zen. His particular style of choice is the Kwan Um School of Zen, of which he is a moderate practitioner. He is always ready to help others and learn new things.

Adam is the founder of DragonPoe.com and RussianPoe.com. He is also running a Slack channel to discuss creative writing with like-minded people.

88153193R00022

Made in the USA
San Bernardino, CA
10 September 2018